This book belongs to:

This edition first published in 2001 by Brown Watson
The Old Mill, 76 Fleckney Road,
Kibworth Beauchamp,
Leicestershire, England.

A Magical Night Before Christmas

A Visit from St. Nicholas
By Clement C. Moore

Brown Watson
ENGLAND

'Twas the night before Christmas,
when all through the house
Not a creature was stirring,
not even a mouse;

The stockings were hung
by the chimney with care,
In hopes that St. Nicholas
soon would be there.

The children were nestled
all snug in their beds,
While visions of sugarplums
danced in their heads;

And mamma in her kerchief,
and I in my cap,
Had just settled our brains
for a long winter nap;

When out on the lawn
   there arose such a clatter,
I sprang from my bed
   to see what was the matter.

Away to the window

I flew like a flash,

Tore open the shutters

and threw up the sash.

The moon, on the breast
of the new-fallen snow,
Gave a lustre of midday
to objects below,

When, what to my wondering
eyes should appear,
But a miniature sleigh
and eight tiny reindeer,

With a little old driver
so lively and quick,
I knew in a moment
it must be St. Nick.

More rapid than eagles,

his coursers they came,

And he whistled and shouted

and called them by name:

"Now, Dasher! Now, Dancer!
Now, Prancer and Vixen!

On Comet! On Cupid!
On Donner and Blitzen!
To the top of the porch,
to the top of the wall,

Now, dash away! Dash away!

Dash away all!"

As dry leaves that before

the wild hurricane fly,

When they meet with an obstacle,

mount to the sky,

So up to the housetop
the coursers they flew,
With the sleigh full of toys,
and St. Nicholas, too.

And then, in a twinkling,

I heard on the roof

The prancing and pawing

of each little hoof.

As I drew in my head,

and was turning around,

Down the chimney St. Nicholas

came with a bound.

He was dressed all in fur

from his head to his foot,

And his clothes were all tarnished

with ashes and soot;

A bundle of toys
    he had flung on his back,
And he looked like a pedlar
    just opening his pack.

His eyes – how they twinkled!
    His dimples – how merry!
His cheeks were like roses,
    his nose like a cherry.

His droll little mouth

was drawn up like a bow,

And the beard on his chin

was as white as the snow.

He had a broad face
  and a little round belly
That shook when he laughed
  like a bowlful of jelly.

He was chubby and plump,
a right jolly old elf,
And I laughed when I saw him
in spite of myself.

A wink of his eye

    and a twist of his head

Soon gave me to know

    I had nothing to dread.

He spoke not a word,
but went straight to his work,
And filled all the stockings;
then turned with a jerk,

And laying his finger

aside of his nose,

And giving a nod,

up the chimney he rose.

He sprang to his sleigh,
to his team gave a whistle
And away they all flew
like the down of a thistle.

But I heard him exclaim,
   'ere he drove out of sight,
"Happy Christmas to all,
   and to all a good night!"